Rocket the Brave!

For Charlie and Elinor,
who never let fear get
in their way

Copyright © 2018 by Tad Hills

All rights reserved. Published in the United States by Schwartz & Wade Books, an imprint of
Random House Children's Books, a division of Penguin Random House LLC, New York.
Schwartz & Wade Books and the colophon are trademarks of Penguin Random House LLC.

Visit us on the Web!
rhcbooks.com
Educators and librarians, for a variety of teaching tools, visit us at RHTeachersLibrarians.com

Library of Congress Cataloging-in-Publication Data
Name: Hills, Tad, author, illustrator.
Title: Rocket the brave / Tad Hills.
Description: First edition. | New York : Schwartz & Wade Books, [2018] |
Summary: Rocket the dog has fun chasing a butterfly up a hill and around a pond, but he does
not want to follow it into the scary forest.
Identifiers: LCCN 2017022882 | ISBN 978-1-5247-7346-5 (hardcover) | ISBN 978-1-5247-7347-2
(trade paperback) | ISBN 978-1-5247-7348-9 (library bound) | ISBN 978-1-5247-7349-6 (ebook)
Subjects: | CYAC: Courage—Fiction. | Butterflies—Fiction. | Dogs—Fiction.
Classification: LCC PZ7.H563737 Rm 2018 | DDC [E]—dc23

The text of this book is set in 24-point Century.
The illustrations were rendered in colored pencils and acrylic paint.

MANUFACTURED IN CHINA

10 9 8 7 6 5 4 3 2 1

Rocket the Brave!

Tad Hills

schwartz & wade books · new york

There is a butterfly

on Rocket's nose.

"Hello, butterfly,"
says Rocket.

He wags his tail.

The butterfly flies away.

"Wait," Rocket says.

Rocket is fast.

The butterfly is faster.

The butterfly flies
up the hill.

Rocket runs
up the hill.

The butterfly flies
past the pond.

Rocket runs
past the pond.

The butterfly rests
on a flower.

Rocket rests, too.

The butterfly flies off.

"Wait!" Rocket says.

The butterfly flies
into the forest.

Rocket stops.

The forest is very dark.

The trees are very tall.

Rocket does not
want to go
into the forest.

"The forest is
very scary,"
he says to himself.

Rocket thinks
for a moment.

The butterfly
was not afraid
to go
into the forest.

The butterfly was brave.

Maybe the forest
is not scary.

Rocket walks

into the forest.

It is very dark.

It is very quiet.

There are many
tall trees.

There are

pinecones,

and ferns,

and ...

the butterfly!

"Hello, butterfly,"
says Rocket.

The forest is
not so scary
after all.

Rocket likes the forest.

Rocket is brave.